For Walter Robinson and Dennis Reaser—
you was both real good teachers

This paperback edition first published in Great Britain in 2016 by Andersen Press Ltd.,
20 Vauxhall Bridge Road, London SW1V 2SA.
Published by special arrangement with Houghton Mifflin Harcourt Publishing Company, and
Rights People, London.
Copyright © Cece Bell, 2015.
The rights of Cece Bell to be identified as the author and illustrator of this work have been
asserted by her in accordance with the Copyright, Designs and Patents Act, 1988.
All rights reserved.
Printed and bound in Malaysia.
British Library cataloguing in Publication Data available.

ISBN 978 1 7 8344 456 4

10  9  8  7  6  5  4  3  2  1

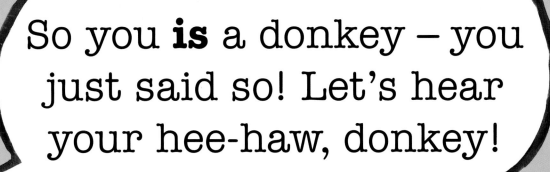

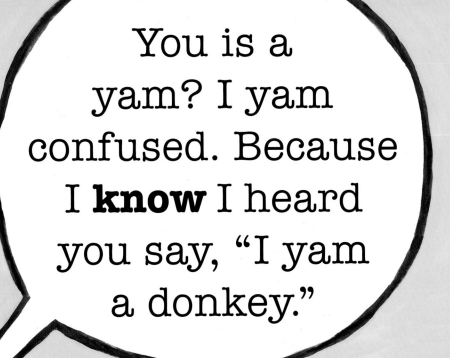

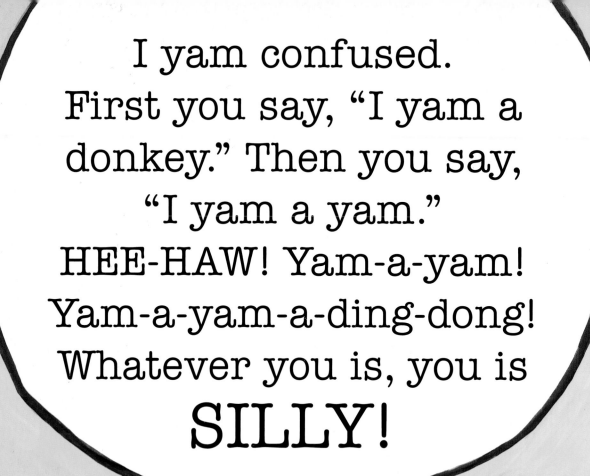

Oh, good grief.
It's not "what is you" –
it's "what **are** you."
What are you, what are you,
what **ARE** you!

What's
going on?

Is **that**
your
hee-haw?
You is the
weirdest
donkey!

Listen, donkey. I am a yam. It's not "I yam" – it's "I **am**." And you are a donkey. It's not "you is" – it's "you **are**."

HUH?

Looks like a big fight about grammar!

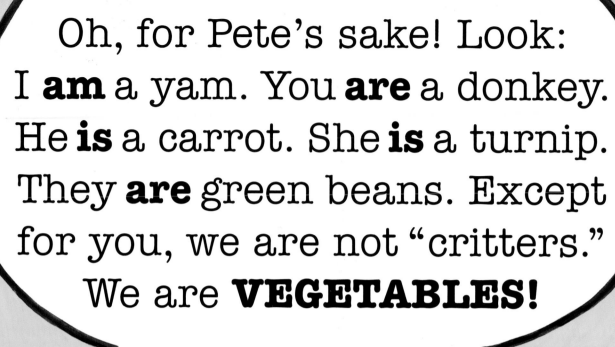

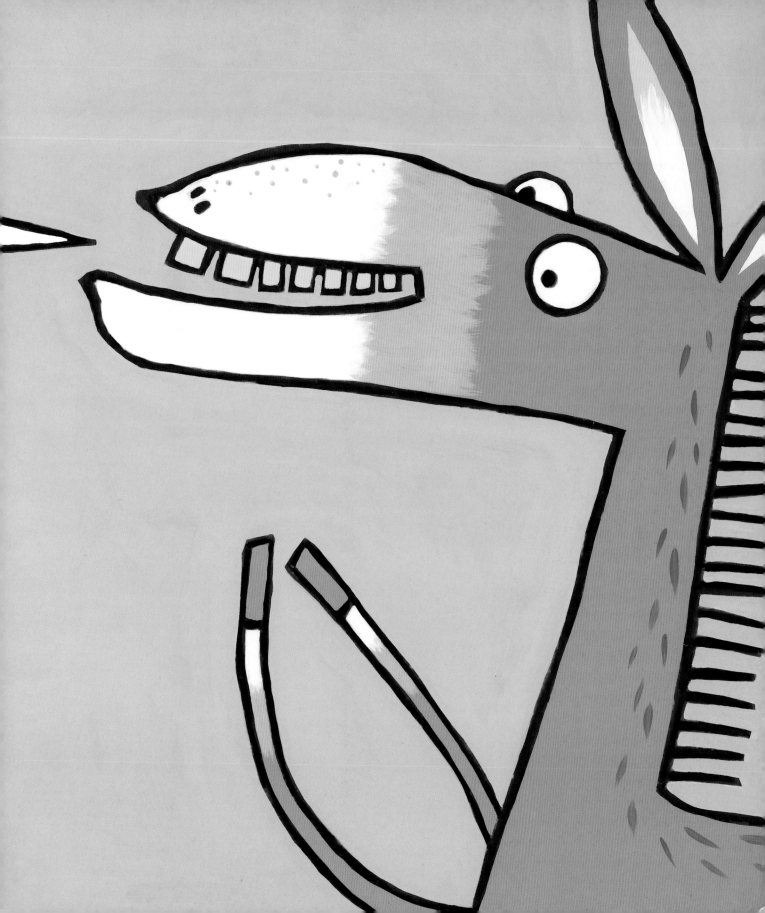

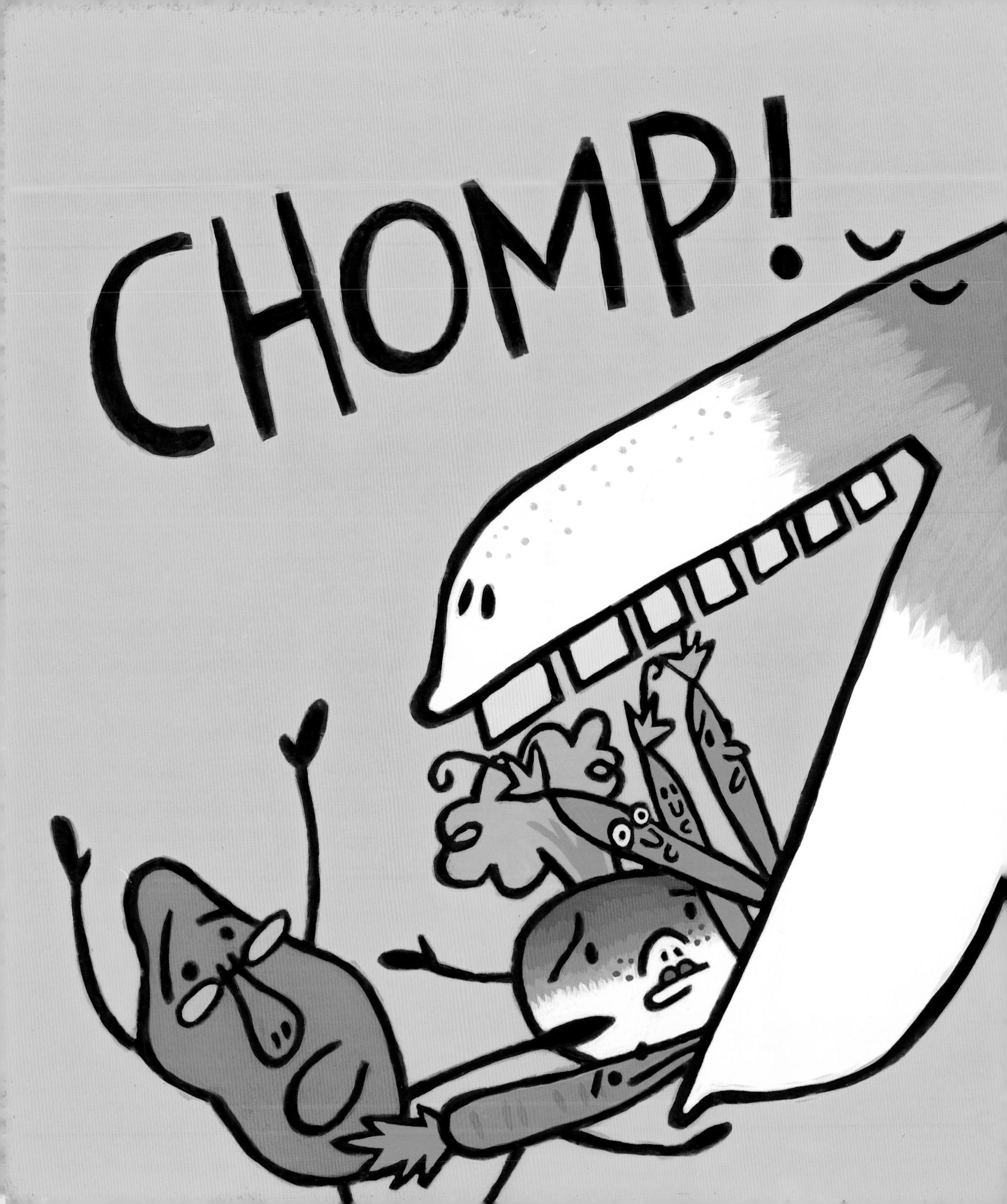
CHOMP!